Oscar Wilde

The happy Prince

retold by Shirley Greenway

pictures by Jane Bottomley

Piccolo Picture Classics

A Piccolo Original

hIGH ABOVE the city, on a tall column, stood the statue of the Happy Prince. He was covered all over with thin layers of fine gold. His eyes were two brilliant sapphires, and a large red ruby glowed on the hilt of his sword.

The statue was very much admired by all the townspeople. 'He is as beautiful as a weathercock,' remarked one of the Town Councillors, to display his good taste. 'Only not quite so useful,' he added, to show that he was also very practical.

'Why can't you be like the Happy Prince?' a mother asked her little boy who was crying for yet another toy. 'The Happy Prince never cries for anything.'

'Well, I am glad there is someone in the world who is perfectly happy,' muttered a disappointed man as he gazed up at the wonderful shining statue.

The children came out of the cathedral all dressed in bright scarlet cloaks and fresh white pinafores. 'He looks just like an angel,' they cried as the Prince's sapphire eyes sparkled in the sunlight.

ONE NIGHT a little Swallow flew over the city. His friends had gone away to Egypt several weeks before but he stayed behind because of his love for a beautiful reed. He had met her early in the spring and had been attracted by her lovely slender form. 'Shall I love you?' asked the Swallow in his direct way. The reed said nothing but made him a low and graceful bow. The Swallow flew round and round her, dipping the tips of his wings into the silver rippling water.

His courtship lasted all summer and he refused to listen to the taunts of the other swallows. In the autumn they all flew away and left him with his lady-love. When he was alone with her he began to find her less exciting – for she never spoke a word to him.

Finally he said: 'Will you come away with me?' But the reed merely shook her head. She would not leave her comfortable river bank.

'Then I am off to the Pyramids. Goodbye!' cried the disappointed Swallow, and away he flew.

ALL THROUGH the day he flew over the land and at night-time he came to the city. He was looking for a place to spend the night when he saw the statue standing on its tall column.

'I will stay here,' he said. 'It is an excellent position with a fine view and plenty of fresh air.' So the little Swallow settled himself between the feet of the Happy Prince. 'I have a golden bedroom,' the Swallow said quietly to himself as he prepared to go to sleep. Suddenly a large drop of water fell on him – and then another.

'How curious!' he cried. 'The sky is clear and bright with stars and yet it is raining. I must find a chimney pot if this statue cannot keep the rain off me.' Just then a third drop fell and he looked up in surprise. The eyes of the Happy Prince were filled with tears – tears which ran down his golden cheeks and fell on to the little Swallow below. His face was so sad and beautiful in the moonlight that the Swallow was filled with pity.

'Who are you?' he asked.

'I am the Happy Prince,' the statue replied.

'Then why are you weeping?'

'When I was alive and had a human heart I never knew what tears were,' the statue answered. 'I lived all my life entirely for pleasure and everyone called me the Happy Prince. But now that I am dead they have set me up here where I can see all the ugliness and misery in my city. Even though my heart is made of lead, yet still I must weep.'

F AR AWAY,' the statue went on in his gentle voice, 'there is a humble house in a little street. By the window sits a poor woman with a thin worn face and busy, needle-pricked fingers. She is a seamstress and she is embroidering a ballgown for the loveliest of the Queen's ladies-in-waiting. In the corner her little boy lies ill with the fever and cries for oranges. Alas, his poor mother has nothing to give him but river water and so he does not get well. Swallow, Swallow, will you not bring her the ruby from my sword-hilt? My feet are fastened here and I cannot move.'

'I am waited for in Egypt,' replied the Swallow. 'Soon all my friends will go to sleep in the tomb of the Great King, who lies there in his painted coffin. I must fly away to join them.'

'Swallow, little Swallow, will you not remain with me for just one night and be my messenger? The boy is so thirsty and his mother is so very worried.'

The Happy Prince looked so sad that the Swallow was sorry he had refused.

'It is very cold here, but I will stay with you for one night and be your messenger.'

'Thank you, little Swallow,' said the Prince.

THE SWALLOW plucked the great ruby from the Prince's sword and flew away with it in his beak over the roofs of the town. When he passed the palace a lovely girl was standing out on the balcony. 'How beautiful the stars are tonight,' remarked her lover, who stood beside her gazing at the sky.

'Oh, I do hope my dress will be ready for the ball, it is to have passion-flowers embroidered all over it,' answered the lady, lost in her own thoughts.

The little Swallow flew on until he reached the humble house in the narrow street. The boy tossed feverishly on his bed while his exhausted mother dozed over her sewing. The Swallow hopped in and laid the ruby on the table. Then he flew gently round the bed cooling the boy's forehead with his wings. When the child settled comfortably to sleep, he flew away again.

He returned to the Happy Prince and told him what he had done. 'It's odd,' he said, 'but I feel quite warm now, although it is so cold.'

'That is because you have done a good action,' said the Prince.

WHEN DAY broke the Swallow flew down to the river for a bath. 'Tonight, I shall go to Egypt,' he said happily to himself. All day long he flew about the town visiting the public buildings and causing much comment. When the moon rose, he flew back to the Happy Prince.

'Now I am off to join my friends in Egypt,' cried the Swallow.

'Swallow, Swallow, little Swallow,' said the Prince sadly. 'Will you not stay with me one night more?'

'But I am waited for in Egypt,' answered the Swallow. 'Tomorrow my friends will fly up to the Second Cataract where sits the God Memnon on a great granite throne, and yellow lions come to the water's edge to drink.'

'Swallow, Swallow, far away across the city I see a young man working in an attic room. He is surrounded by papers but is unable to finish the play he is writing for the Director of the Theatre. There is no fire in the grate and he is so cold and hungry that he can write no more.'

'I will wait one more night,' said the Swallow. 'Shall I take him another ruby?'

'Alas,' said the Prince, 'I have no rubies left, only the sapphires in my eyes. Pluck out one of them and take it quickly to the young man.'

'Dear Prince,' said the Swallow, weeping, 'I cannot do that.'

'Swallow, Swallow, little Swallow, do as I command,' said the Prince firmly. So the Swallow plucked out the Prince's bright eye and, flying swiftly to the attic room, dropped it down among the crumpled paper on the young man's table.

THE NEXT day the Swallow flew down to the bustling harbour. All day he watched the sailors unloading chests out of the hold of a huge ship, and thought about his coming journey to Egypt. At moonrise he flew back to the Happy Prince.

'I have come to bid you goodbye,' he said.

'Swallow, Swallow, little Swallow,' said the Prince, 'Will you not stay with me one night longer?'

'It is winter,' said the Swallow, 'and soon the cold winds will bring the snow. In Egypt it is warm and sunny. Dear Prince, I must leave you but I will never forget you and when I return I shall bring you two beautiful jewels to replace those you have given away.'

'In the square below,' continued the Prince in his quiet voice, 'there stands a little matchgirl. She has no shoes or stockings or cloak, and she has dropped her matches and spoiled them. Pluck out my other eye and bring it to her.'

'I will stay with you one night longer,' answered the Swallow, with a sigh, 'but I cannot pluck out your eye, for then you would be blind!'

'Swallow, Swallow, little Swallow,' said the Prince, 'do as I command you.'

So he plucked out the Prince's other eye and darted down to where the little matchgirl stood weeping. He swooped past and dropped the jewel into her hand. The girl laughed to see how the pretty thing sparkled in the light.

THE SWALLOW flew back to the Prince. 'You are blind now and so I will stay with you always,' he said.

'No, little Swallow,' answered the sad Prince, 'you must fly away to Egypt and the sun.'

'I will stay with you always,' repeated the Swallow, and he slept that night at the feet of the Prince.

All through the day the Swallow sat on the Prince's shoulder and told him stories of strange lands. He spoke of the red ibises who stand in long rows on the banks of the Nile, catching goldfish in their beaks; of the Sphinx who lives in the desert and is as old and wise as time itself. He spoke of the merchants who walk slowly beside their camels and carry amber beads in their hands, and of the great green snake that sleeps in a palm tree where twenty priests feed him with honey-cakes.

'Dear little Swallow,' said the Prince, 'you tell me of such wonderful things, but what I really wish to know about are the sufferings of my own people. Fly out over the city, little Swallow, and tell me what you see there.'

O THE SWALLOW flew out over the great city and saw the lives of both the rich and the poor. There was much misery. The Swallow returned each day and told the Prince of everything he had seen – of the dark lanes and of starving children with pinched faces, of beggars and poor widows.

'I am covered with the finest gold,' said the Prince. 'You must take it off leaf by leaf and give it to all the poor people. Perhaps it will make them happy.'

Leaf by leaf the Swallow plucked the gold, until the Prince looked grey and shabby, and leaf by leaf he brought the gold to the poor people and they were able to buy food and clothing. The children's faces grew rosy and they laughed and played games in the streets.

Then the snow fell and the frosts came. The streets glistened hard and bright. The rich people put on their furs and boys in scarlet caps skated on the ice.

The poor Swallow grew colder and colder but he loved the Prince and would not leave his side. He picked up the crumbs outside the baker's door when the baker wasn't looking, and tried in vain to keep himself warm by flapping his wings.

AT LAST THE little Swallow knew that he was going to die. He had just enough strength to fly up once more and perch on the Prince's shoulder.

'Goodbye, dear Prince!' he said softly.

'I am glad that you are going to Egypt at last, little Swallow,' said the Prince, 'you have already stayed too long. But you must kiss me goodbye before you go.'

'It is not to Egypt that I am going,' replied the little Swallow, 'but to Death, the brother of sleep.' Then he kissed the Happy Prince goodbye, and fell down dead at his feet.

Suddenly a curious crack came from inside the statue. The Prince's leaden heart had snapped in two – it certainly was a dreadfully hard frost.

EARLY THE next morning the Mayor and the Town Councillors were walking in the square. As they passed the column where the statue stood, the Mayor looked up at the Happy Prince.

'Dear me, how shabby our Prince has become,' he cried. 'He has lost the ruby from his sword, his eyes are gone and he is golden no longer. He looks no better than a beggar!'

'. . . just like a beggar!' echoed the Town Councillors.

'And there is actually a dead bird lying at his base!' the Mayor continued. 'We really must issue a proclamation that birds are not allowed to die here!'

As the statue was no longer beautiful they had it pulled down and melted in a great furnace. 'We shall use the metal to make a new statue,' declared the Mayor, 'and it shall be of myself!'

'. . . of myself, of myself,' repeated the Town Councillors.

However, at the metal foundry the foreman made a strange discovery. 'This broken lead heart will not melt in the furnace! We must throw it away.' And so they tossed the Prince's leaden heart on to the rubbish-heap – where it lay next to the body of a small dead swallow.

'Bring me the two most precious things in the city,'
said God to one of his Angels. The Angel flew down
to the rubbish-heap and brought back the leaden
heart and the dead bird.

'You have chosen wisely,' God said, 'and in my city
of gold the Happy Prince shall praise me while the
little Swallow sings his song in Paradise for ever-
more.'